*"A lovely tale, simply told, showing the value of friendship,
with a message of hope for all of us."*
Steve Howey, Richard House Children's Hospice, www.richardhouseorg.uk

*"A lovely wee read about Peanut and Paul and their unique connection.
The beautiful illustration supports the tale wonderfully."*
Louise Russell, www.giveadogabone.net

Tay comes in so many sizes!
Love, Molly xxx

PEANUT THE HAMSTER

ISBN: 978-1-917022-13-2

Edit & layout Shaun Russell

Published by
Candy Jar Books
Mackintosh House
136 Newport Road, Cardiff, CF24 1DJ
www.candyjarbooks.co.uk

Printed and bound in the UK by
4edge, 22 Eldon Way, Hockley, Essex, SS5 4AD

PEANUT THE HAMSTER

MOLLY ARBUTHNOTT

Illustrated by Anastasiia Morozova

Peanut was a hamster. He was furry, had four legs, a big tummy and his favourite food was… you guessed it… peanuts! He had a birthmark the shape of a peanut on his back too and so was nutty through and through.

He travelled everywhere with his owner, Paul who was equally nutty (in mind rather than looks) in the most endearing way. Paul and Peanut were inseparable. They needed each other like Beauty needed the Beast and Lady needed the Tramp.

Paul was a very famous author, a prolific author, with an apparent treasure trove of ideas. Only Peanut and Paul knew the truth though.

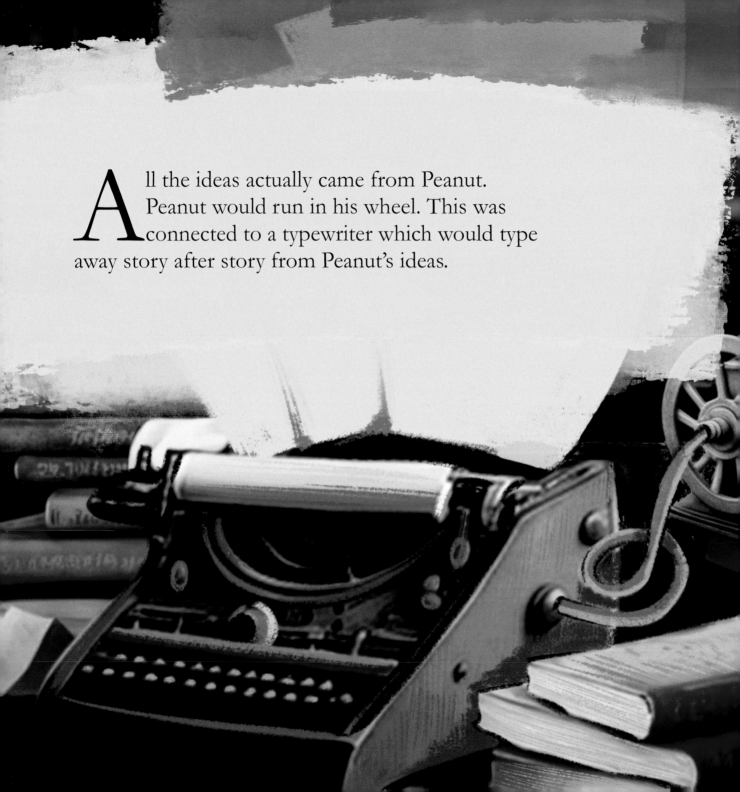

All the ideas actually came from Peanut. Peanut would run in his wheel. This was connected to a typewriter which would type away story after story from Peanut's ideas.

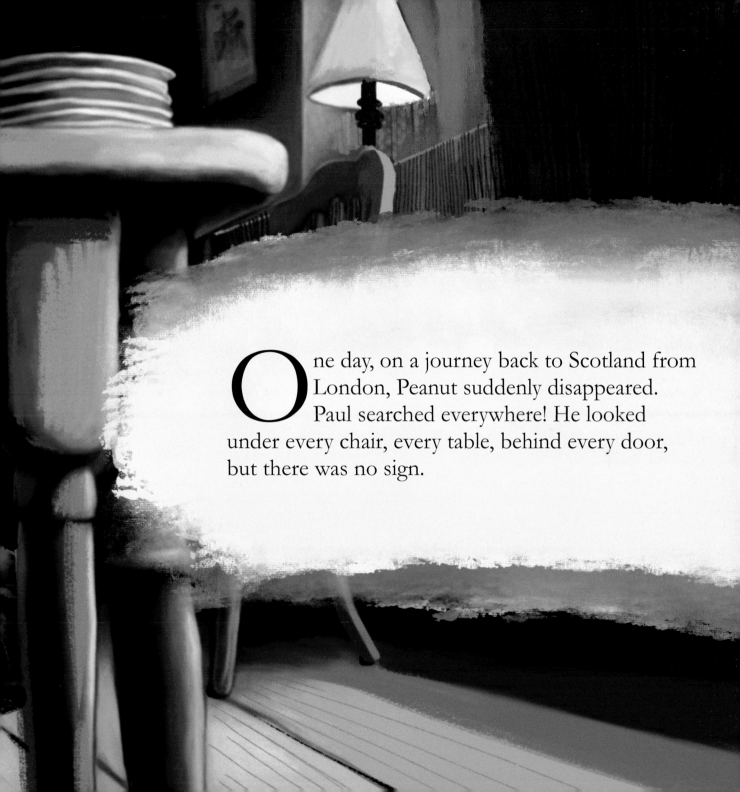

One day, on a journey back to Scotland from London, Peanut suddenly disappeared. Paul searched everywhere! He looked under every chair, every table, behind every door, but there was no sign.

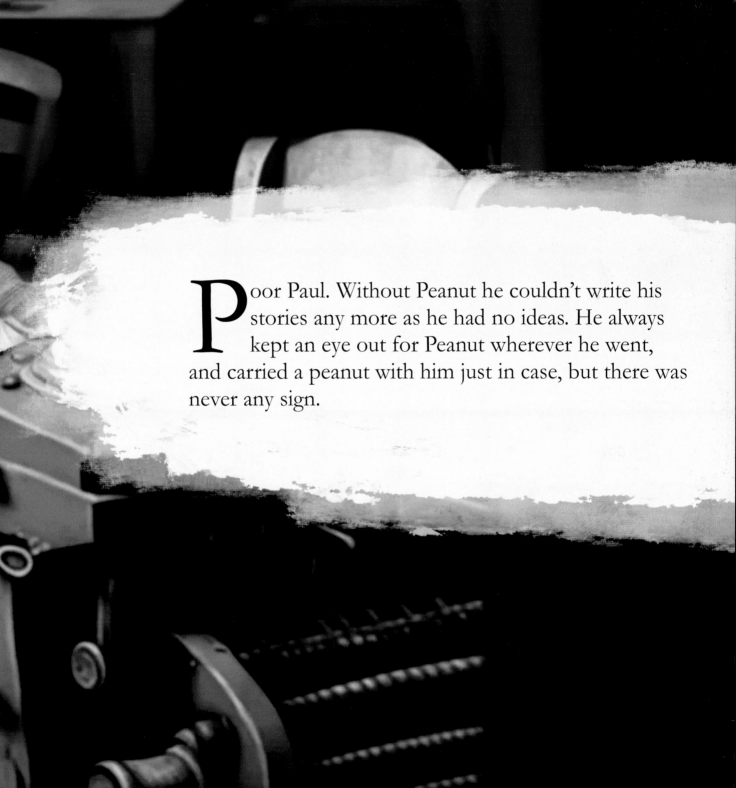

Poor Paul. Without Peanut he couldn't write his stories any more as he had no ideas. He always kept an eye out for Peanut wherever he went, and carried a peanut with him just in case, but there was never any sign.

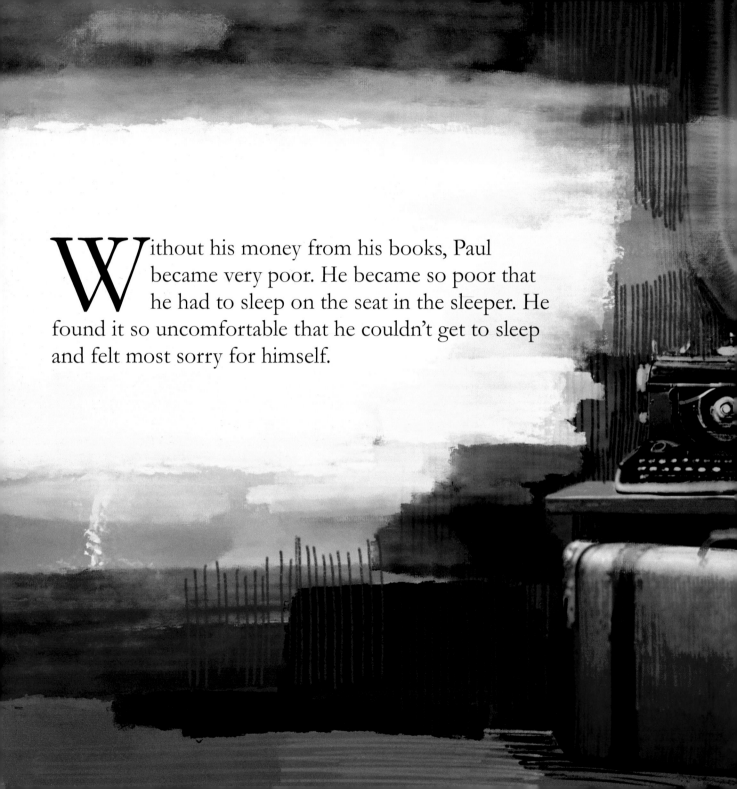

Without his money from his books, Paul became very poor. He became so poor that he had to sleep on the seat in the sleeper. He found it so uncomfortable that he couldn't get to sleep and felt most sorry for himself.

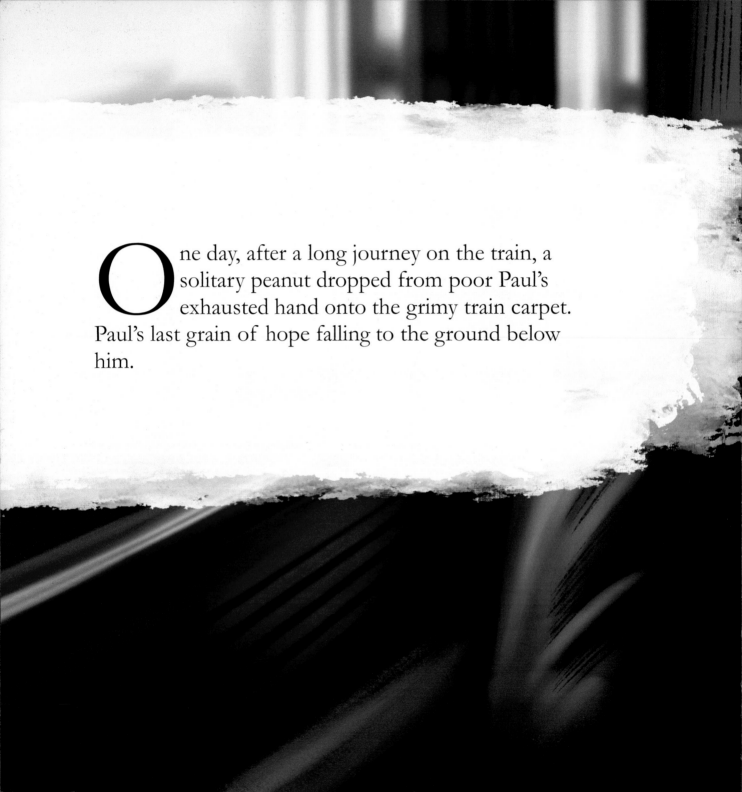

One day, after a long journey on the train, a solitary peanut dropped from poor Paul's exhausted hand onto the grimy train carpet. Paul's last grain of hope falling to the ground below him.

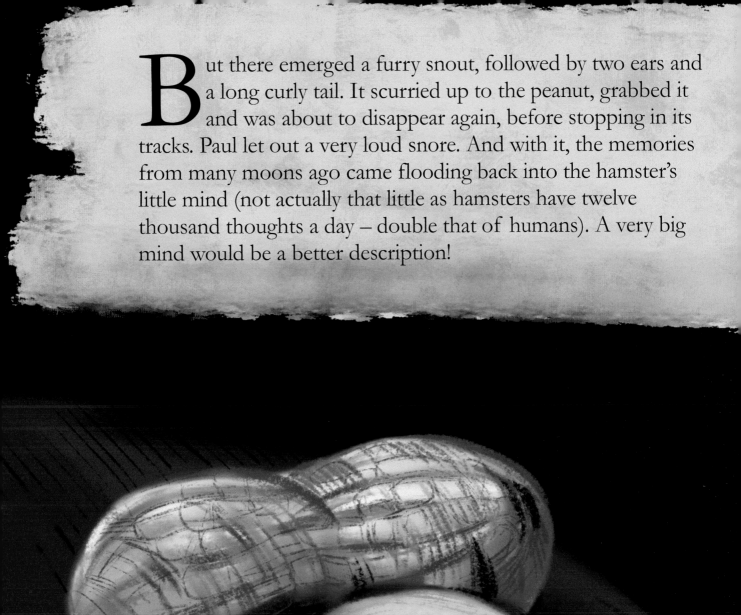

But there emerged a furry snout, followed by two ears and a long curly tail. It scurried up to the peanut, grabbed it and was about to disappear again, before stopping in its tracks. Paul let out a very loud snore. And with it, the memories from many moons ago came flooding back into the hamster's little mind (not actually that little as hamsters have twelve thousand thoughts a day – double that of humans). A very big mind would be a better description!

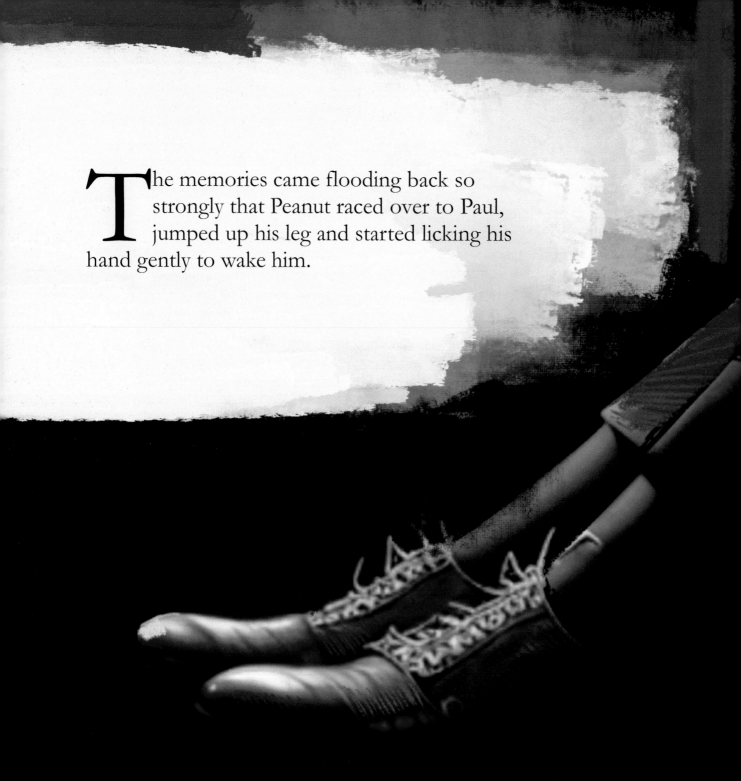

The memories came flooding back so strongly that Peanut raced over to Paul, jumped up his leg and started licking his hand gently to wake him.

Paul woke with a start and couldn't quite believe his eyes. Many years had passed since he had last set eyes on Peanut, but his friend looked the same, a bit greyer around the whiskers, but he could still see the peanut birthmark. There was no doubt in Paul's mind.

Peanut hopped onto the ground and raced out the door before returning to Paul, as if he wanted Paul to follow him.

Paul pulled himself out of his seat and followed Peanut out the door, and down the corridor towards the warm kitchen. There, in a little hole near the oven, was Peanut's family!

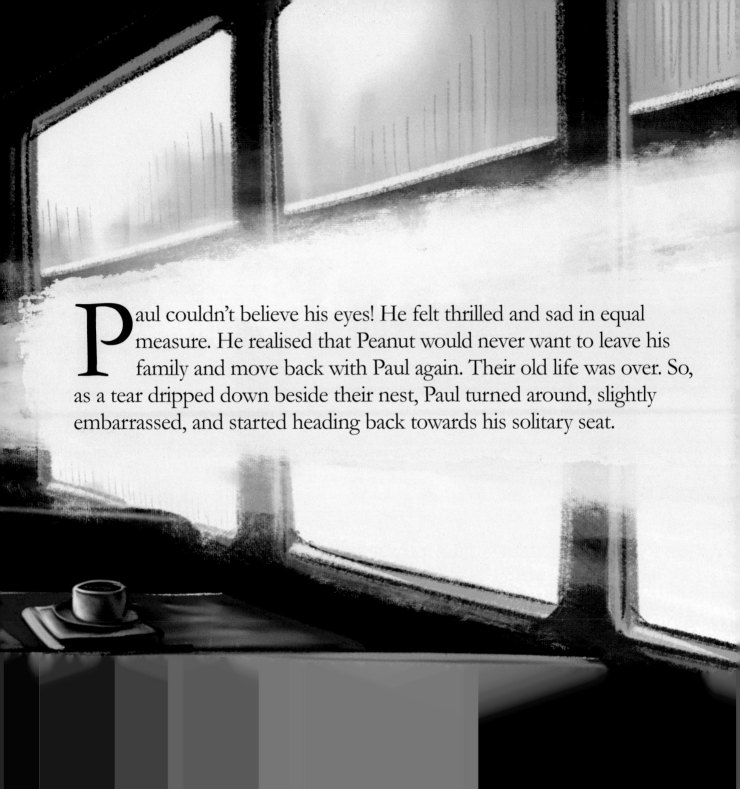

Paul couldn't believe his eyes! He felt thrilled and sad in equal measure. He realised that Peanut would never want to leave his family and move back with Paul again. Their old life was over. So, as a tear dripped down beside their nest, Paul turned around, slightly embarrassed, and started heading back towards his solitary seat.

He was sitting down drying his eyes. Just as he was about to go back to sleep, Peanut suddenly hopped up onto his knee. Peanut had a peanut in his hands, which he nibbled. He then passed carefully on to Paul, before scurrying away. Paul wasn't too sure about a half nibbled peanut. *Quite some parting gift*, he thought. But he duly ate the nut and… whoosh!

He could write!
What power had passed on to him!

He got a pen and some paper and started writing. Once he started he just couldn't stop. The power in the peanut had transferred all of Peanut's story ideas to Paul.

So, if you're ever stuck for an idea, try eating a peanut and maybe, just maybe, it will be a magical one full of amazing story ideas too!